DAVID ROBERTS'
DELIGHTFULLY DIFFERENT FAIRY TALES

First published in the UK in 2020 by
Pavilion Books Company Limited
43 Great Ormond Street
London, WC1N 3HZ

Publisher: Neil Dunnicliffe
Designer: Gemma Doyle

ISBN: 9781843654759

A CIP catalogue record for this book is available from the British Library.

10 9 8 7 6 5 4 3 2 1

Reproduction by Rival Colour Ltd., UK
Printed and bound by Toppan Leefung Ltd, China

This book can be ordered at www.pavilionbooks.com, or try your local bookshop.

MIX
Paper from
responsible sources
FSC
www.fsc.org   FSC® C104723

DAVID ROBERTS'
DELIGHTFULLY
DIFFERENT
FAIRY TALES

LYNN ROBERTS-MALONEY

Introduction

I was so excited to be asked to illustrate these classic fairy tales. I love how a fairy tale can be interpreted in a variety of ways!

Working with my sister was a great privilege and a new and interesting creative process. We combined our imaginations, thinking of visual ways to tell each story, setting them in unexpected time periods.

Each story influenced the setting, like Rapunzel living in a high-rise flat, and in turn each of the settings influenced the retelling of the story, like Sleeping Beauty pricking her finger on a record player's needle.

Researching the time periods for each book was a great pleasure, taking me from the jazz age and art deco aesthetic of the 1920s and '30s, through the 1950s mid-century modern style and rock and roll fashions, to the platform shoes, high-rise flats and music of the 1970s.

I really hope you enjoy stepping back in time with Greta, Annabel and Rapunzel.

David Roberts

Contents

CINDERELLA

An art deco fairy tale

RAPUNZEL

A groovy 1970s fairy tale

SLEEPING BEAUTY

A mid-century fairy tale

For Mum and Dad

Cinderella

An art deco fairy tale

In a time not too long ago and in a land much like our own, there lived a young and beautiful girl. Her name was Greta. She lived alone with her father because her mother had died many years before.

Greta's father was a kind man. He could be quite forgetful and could not see anything at all without his glasses. One day he gathered up his papers and set off for the city to attend an important meeting. "Goodbye, Greta dear, I shall be back in two days," he called. When he finally returned after two *weeks*, he had a big surprise.

In the city he had met a woman whose beauty was such that it could only be recognized by a few (particularly those who had lost their glasses). He married the woman straight away in a church that was cold and hard, rather like his new wife's heart. She had two daughters, Elvira and Ermintrude. Elvira was as wicked as Ermintrude was dim, and Ermintrude was very, very dim.

When her new stepmother saw Greta's fine clothes and jewels, she said, "My girls should have some of these. You do not need them all." Elvira and Ermintrude fought over every piece and left Greta with only one simple frock.

"Greta, your room is perfect for my girls. You can find another," her stepmother said smugly.

So Greta was forced to sleep in the kitchen. At night she lay by the fire to keep warm. When she wakened she was always covered in dust and cinders. Elvira and Ermintrude started calling her "Cinderella", and soon even her father called her by that name. He thought it was just a friendly endearment.

One day, as she was cleaning the house, Cinderella heard an announcement on the radio. She ran to tell her stepmother and stepsisters the exciting news. "The king is to hold a ball in honour of his son, Prince Roderick," Cinderella explained breathlessly. "All the eligible girls in the land are invited. The prince is going to choose a bride!"

There was great excitement on the day of the ball. Cinderella's stepmother knew that Cinderella's beauty outshone that of her own daughters. To make sure Cinderella had no time to prepare for the ball, she made her run back and forth helping Elvira and Ermintrude.

"Brush my hair, Cinderella!" shouted Ermintrude.

"Bring my grey dress," snarled Elvira. "And do my make-up!"

Alone in the kitchen, Cinderella sighed and wiped away a tear as she watched the sisters and their mother drive away in all their finery.

Suddenly a bright light filled the kitchen, and a kindly woman appeared.

"Do not be frightened," the woman said. "You *shall* go to the ball. Go outside and fetch a stout grey rat, a large leek, four white mice and two glow-worms, and leave them on the drive. Be quick, as we do not have much time."

Cinderella did as she was told. Then the kindly lady closed her eyes and said:

"Magic, magic, work on all:

Get Cinderella to the ball!"

A rumble was heard. Then a flash of light revealed a chauffeur standing in front of a gleaming white car. Cinderella found that her rags had changed into a beautiful gown, and on her feet were glass slippers.

"You are ready," said the kindly lady. "But beware! You must be home before midnight." With that she disappeared. Cinderella climbed into the car and sped off to the ball.

The ball was already in full swing when Cinderella crept in, anxious in case her stepsisters recognized her.

"This is hopeless," Prince Roderick muttered to himself as he prepared to leave. "There is no one here whom I find interesting." Then his eyes fell on Cinderella. In an instant he fell in love.

The prince took Cinderella's hand and led her to the dance floor. They danced together for the rest of the evening and everyone – even her stepsisters – wondered who the beautiful girl could be. Then the clock began to strike midnight. Cinderella, remembering the kindly woman's warning, raced to the door. As she ran down the palace steps, her beautiful clothes began to turn into rags. In her haste she lost one delicate glass slipper on the stairs, but she managed to slip the other into her pocket.

In the car park Cinderella found her leek, rat, mice and glow-worms where the car and chauffeur had been. Gathering them up, she ran home as fast as she could.

Prince Roderick held Cinderella's dainty glass slipper in his hand. "The girl whose foot fits this slipper shall be my bride!" he vowed. He knew that he could never love another.

The next morning, breakfast was interrupted by another announcement on the radio: the prince planned to visit every girl in the land that very day to find the stranger with whom he had danced.

Cinderella's stepmother did not know that Cinderella had been at the ball, but she did not want to take any chances. She was determined that the prince would not see Cinderella's beauty.

"Go and do the laundry," she ordered, to get Cinderella out of the way.

Meanwhile, Elvira and Ermintrude prepared themselves for the royal visit.

At last the prince arrived. After greeting him, Elvira tried the shoe on, but her foot was too wide. Then Ermintrude pushed her foot into the tiny shoe. For one moment it looked as though it might fit ... but her foot was too long.

"Why not let Cinderella try?" asked her father, coming into the room.

"She was not even at the ball," her stepmother snapped. But the prince saw a familiar pair of eyes peeping out from behind a screen. To the horror of Cinderella's stepmother and stepsisters, Prince Roderick took Cinderella by the hand and led her to the couch. He slipped the shoe on to her foot.

"A perfect fit!" he cried. Cinderella pulled the other shoe from her pocket, and the prince knew that he had found his bride.

Cinderella (for she kept her new name) and her prince were married soon after. Because she had a forgiving nature, Cinderella allowed Ermintrude and Elvira to attend the wedding. And they *almost* managed to behave themselves.

Illustrator's Note

When I was asked to illustrate *Cinderella,* I thought it would be interesting to set the story in the 1930s. I have always had an interest in that period and wanted to incorporate art deco designs alongside those of earlier periods. My background in fashion design made it especially fun to research the wardrobe for Cinderella and her wicked stepfamily. In creating these characters, I was influenced by the movie stars, magazine covers, and art of the 1920s and '30s. The paintings that decorate the walls are my humble interpretations of those by Augustus John and Tamara de Lempicka, and the wallpaper, furniture, and pottery are all based on real art deco designs.

The illustrations were done in pen and ink with watercolour on hot pressed, heavyweight paper.

For
Grandad Burns and Grandad Roberts
and to the memory of
Nana Jean Burns and
Grandma Anne "Queenie" Roberts

Rapunzel

**A groovy 1970s
fairy tale**

In a time not too long ago and in a land much like our own, there lived a very beautiful girl with the most extraordinarily long red hair.

Her name was Rapunzel and she lived with her Aunt Edna and Roach, Edna's hideous pet crow. Rapunzel had been brought up by Edna after her parents died when she was very young. Edna kept her locked up so she could not go out and enjoy herself.

To keep Rapunzel quiet (and to make herself seem nice, which she was not) Edna brought Rapunzel second-hand magazines and records and occasionally allowed her to watch television. "When you are older," Edna lied, "I'll take you out and show you the city, but it's not safe for you on your own."

Rapunzel believed every word, for she knew nothing of the world.

The tower block they lived in was old and deserted. The lift was always broken and there were hundreds of stairs to the ground. This was not a problem for Aunt Edna as she had a special way of entering and leaving the building.

Rapunzel would hang her plait over the balcony and Edna would climb down it. On her return she would shout, "Rapunzel, Rapunzel, let down your hair!" Then, Rapunzel would throw her long plait over the balcony, Edna would grab hold, and Rapunzel would slowly pull her up.

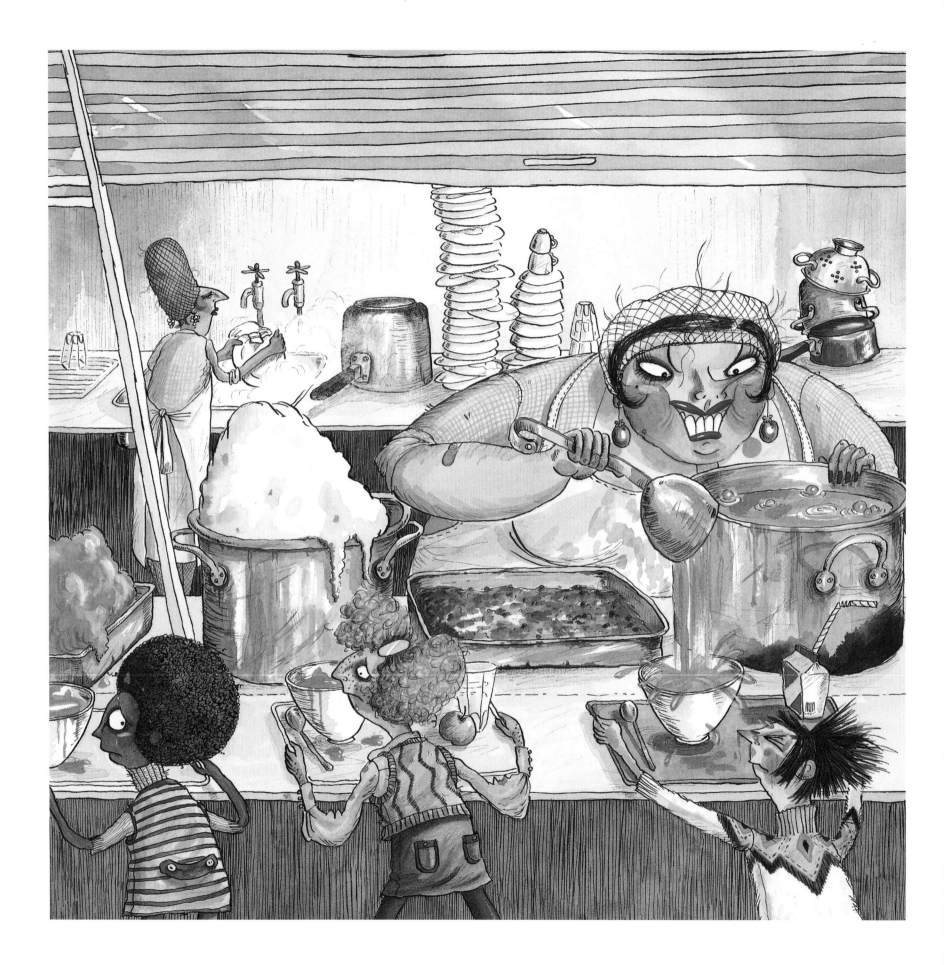

Aunt Edna worked at the local school. She was the most fearsome dinner lady the children had ever seen. Prowling around the canteen, she would force them to eat every scrap of food, even cold pea soup and lumpy custard. Edna also trained Roach to swoop down and steal things from the children to bring to her. Edna selfishly took all the best things and gave the scarves and jewellery she didn't like to Rapunzel, pretending she had bought them.

One morning, as Aunt Edna struggled down Rapunzel's hair,

a boy who had stopped to fix his bike on the way to school

happened to see this extraordinary sight. His name was Roger and

he was the singer in the local school band, Roger and the Rascals.

Intrigued, he thought, "Surely that's the nasty dinner lady from

school! What is she doing?"

After school, he raced back to the tower block. To his astonishment,

he heard the nasty dinner lady booming out, "Rapunzel, Rapunzel, let

down your hair!" Seeing

the beautiful red plait

tumble over the

balcony, Roger

knew he had to

meet the girl with

the long hair.

The next day was Saturday, and Roger could not wait to go back. Luckily for him, Edna was just on her way to a much-needed fitness class.

Roger took a deep breath and, trying his best to imitate Edna's booming voice, he called, "Rapunzel, Rapunzel, let down your hair!" To his amazement, the rope of hair was lowered. Hesitantly Roger took hold of it, then gasped as he was lifted into the air.

As he reached the balcony, he fell over the wall onto all fours.

"Oh my!" Rapunzel exclaimed as she found herself face to face with the most handsome boy she had ever seen.

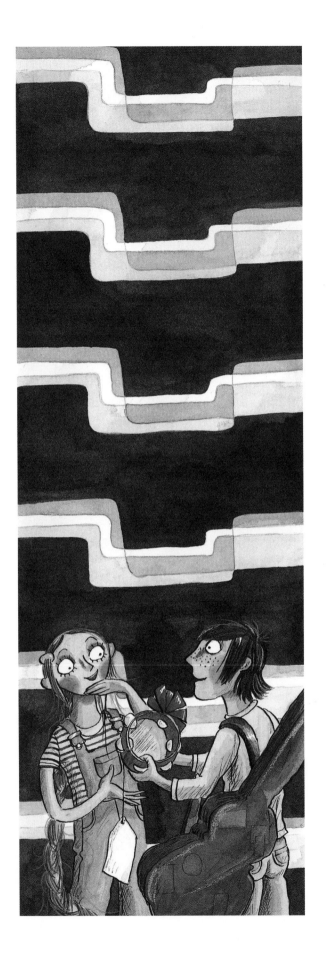

Rapunzel and Roger spent the whole
morning listening to music and talking.

"I feel as if I've known you forever,"
Rapunzel cried, gazing into Roger's eyes.

Every day after this, Roger would wait for
Edna to leave and then visit Rapunzel to say
good morning before he went to school.
He took Rapunzel a present every lunch
time, and sometimes he took along his guitar
so he could sing his new songs for her.
She was happier than she had ever been.

One day, Roger said, "I wish I could find a way to get you out of the flat so that I could show you the city. You can't very well climb down your own hair, and we cannot take the stairs as Edna never forgets to lock the door."

Rapunzel thought for a moment. "I've got a great idea!" she said. "Why don't we make a rope ladder from all the scarves and belts I have?"

Together they set to work.

The very next day, after saying goodbye
to Roger, Rapunzel let her hair down for her
aunt. As Edna reached the top, Rapunzel said
without thinking, "You are so heavy, Aunt. It
is so much easier to pull up my dear Roger."

The moment the words were out, Rapunzel
knew she had spoiled everything.

Edna flew into a rage. She grabbed a pair
of scissors and cut off Rapunzel's long hair.
"How dare you deceive me?" cried Edna as
she forced Rapunzel to climb down her own
hair. "May you never find happiness!" she
screamed. Seething with anger, Edna waited
on the balcony for Roger.

Before long, Roger called to Rapunzel to let down her hair and whistled as he was lifted up, happy at the thought of seeing her again.

But to his horror, when he reached the top, the ugly, twisted face of Edna leered out at him.

"You will never see Rapunzel again," Edna hissed in his ear as she pushed him backwards over the balcony. The hair tumbled with him as he fell to the ground. Wrapped around him, the plait broke his fall, but he banged his head and fell unconscious.

Meanwhile, wandering through the city streets, Rapunzel grew tired and hungry. She found a stray kitten nearly as hungry as she was and called him Rascal after Roger's band. All her life she had wanted to visit the city, but never had she felt more lonely and lost. "Will I ever see Roger again?" she wondered, holding Rascal close.

Roger, however, remembered nothing about
Rapunzel. Dazed from his fall, he staggered home
with the hair he had found wrapped around his
body. He truly had no idea where it had come
from. He put it in his dad's garage which he
used as a studio. "It must mean something," he
puzzled as he practised his guitar.

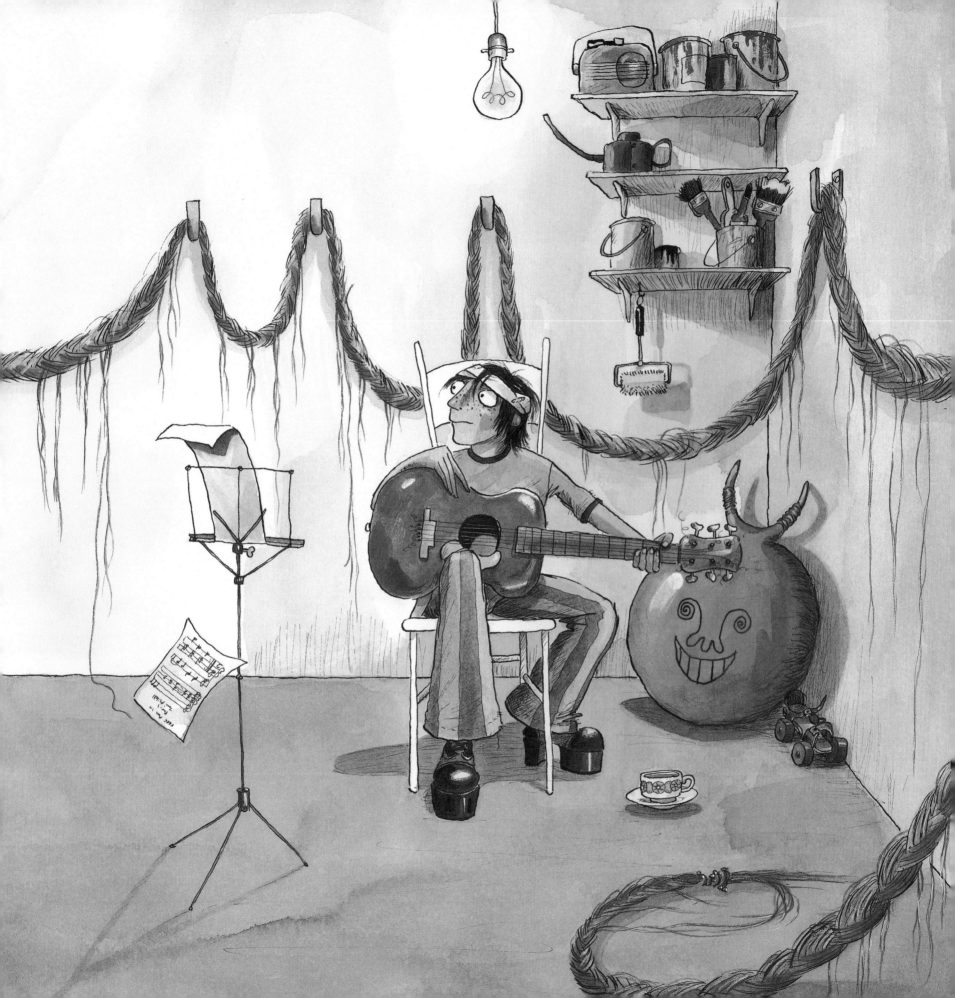

Rapunzel slept in a damp shop doorway that night, with Rascal clasped in her arms. As she awoke, stretching her arms and yawning, she caught sight of a poster. "Roger!" she cried out in surprise. Her beloved Roger and his band were playing a concert at the school that very evening. She would find the school and see Roger again!

Rapunzel could barely contain her excitement when she arrived for the concert. She found a space in the front row just as Roger and his band walked on stage to loud applause. Roger looked out into the crowd and, as he began to sing, his eyes rested on a strangely familiar halo of red hair. And when he looked at Rapunzel's beautiful smiling face, he remembered everything.

Rapunzel and Roger were best friends from that moment on, and as happy as could be. Roger and the Rascals became very successful, playing at every school in town. Rapunzel, deciding to make use of her glorious red hair, learned how to make wigs. She designed them in every style and length imaginable, as long as they were red!

And what happened to Aunt Edna? Well, she no longer had

Rapunzel's hair, and the lift was, of course, out of order...

Illustrator's Note

When I was asked to illustrate a second fairy tale (my first being Cinderella: an art deco fairy tale),
I was very keen to use the story of Rapunzel. At my sister's suggestion, I decided to set the story in a 1970s
tower block, the obvious association with the 1970s being Rapunzel's long hair. As a child growing up at that
time, I was very influenced by the music, films, fashion and design of the period. In researching this book,
I looked at old family photos and magazines to help me remember the clothes and toys I had owned as a child.
I have incorporated record sleeves, film posters, furniture and product design from this period into my
illustrations. I also wanted to link Cinderella to Rapunzel in a subtle way. I imagined the families to be related,
and so a few artefacts from Cinderella have been passed down and found their way into Rapunzel's home.

FOR JOEL AND JOHN

Illustrator's Note

I was so excited to be working with my sister Lynn on another fairy tale retelling. We decided on Sleeping Beauty because we wanted to play around with time, and explore how we could represent the passage of 1000 years! We both loved the films and TV shows of the 1950s that looked at a futuristic world. From robots to aliens, space ships to flying cars the mid-century view of the future was full of style and innovation. We both thought it would be great fun to show Sleeping Beauty wake after her 1000-year sleep into a world that looked very much like the one she had dreamed about as a teenager in the 1950s.

The '50s was a great time for music too and particularly music aimed at a young audience. This gave us the perfect opportunity to switch the spinning wheel spindle in the original story to a record player needle, on which Annabel pricks her finger.

The wicked fairy is inspired by the Disney villains I grew up watching. She wears green in homage to a number of Disney film counterparts.

I had got very tired of the set formula of a fairy tale with its male hero "rescuing" the female character and was keen to change that set up for our version. Lynn was very much in agreement and in the end removed all the male characters from the story, instead giving us Zoe, the intrepid library-loving, history-obsessed teenage hero who breaks the sleeping spell cast on Annabel.

SLEEPING BEAUTY

A MID-CENTURY FAIRY TALE

In a time not too long ago and in a land much like our own,

there was a happy young girl called Annabel. She lived with her two aunts,

Rosalind and Flora. Annabel loved science fiction and spent hours dreaming

of the future, unaware that she was living under an evil spell that could mean

she had no future at all.

On Annabel's first birthday something had happened to change her future forever. All the neighbours were invited to a party, but one of them was a mean and spiteful witch called Morwenna. She was jealous of Rosalind, Flora and the beautiful baby Annabel, so she set out to spoil the fun.

All the guests fussed over baby Annabel and gave her gifts. They were having a wonderful time until Morwenna stepped forward.

"Here's *my* gift" she cried, casting a spell. "Before her 16th birthday is over, she will prick her finger on a needle and die!" In a flash Morwenna disappeared, leaving behind only the echo of an evil laugh.

Rosalind cried in despair, afraid that she could do nothing to stop the spell from coming true. But Flora, who was a good and kind witch, said "Morwenna is powerful and her spell is strong. I can't take the spell away… but I can change it. If Annabel pricks her finger she will not die, but will sleep for a thousand years."

To avoid upsetting Rosalind further, Flora kept a secret. Morwenna's spell was so strong that if Annabel was not woken at exactly midnight on the last day of the thousand years she would indeed die.

Rosalind removed every needle from their home and kept a careful watch over Annabel. Oblivious to her fate, Annabel spent her time reading space books and watching television. She marvelled at the films and stories about science and robots. She often thought that if she could wish for anything, it would be to see the world as it is in the future.

Annabel's 16th birthday arrived. Rosalind was so relieved that Annabel would be 16 and the spell would be lifted that she let her guard down and did not notice that a large present wrapped in shiny paper had been delivered to the house.

Annabel excitedly tore off the paper. Inside was a record player. This was something Annabel had desperately wanted but had not been allowed to have. "It must be a surprise gift from my aunts," she thought happily.

But it wasn't from her aunts. Morwenna had left the gift, and she spied

through the window as Annabel put the record on. In her excitement Annabel

pricked her finger on the needle. In an instant she fell to the floor asleep.

The spell had come true.

When Rosalind found Annabel she was inconsolable. "How will I protect her? I cannot watch over her for 1000 years," she sobbed. Flora had an idea.

"Rosalind become a rose
Do not shed any tears
Grow with magic, grow with love
Guard Annabel for a thousand years."

In a shimmer of golden light Rosalind began to change. She became a rose tree, which grew and grew. Out of the windows and doors thick vines and thorns entwined to leave no sign of what lay beneath. Flora wrote down the story so that it would never be forgotten. She called it *Sleeping Beauty*. She then turned herself into a light, so Annabel was not in darkness.

Many, many years went by and the world saw many changes

but the rose tree remained.

A thousand years passed and a young girl called Zoe was researching the history of the giant rose tree. She wondered why it still stood when everything around it had changed so much. She set off to the library to find out more.

In the library Zoe found a collection of very old and dusty books. She loved books and history and finding out about what life used to be like. She often thought that if she could wish for anything, it would be to see the world as it was in the past.

Zoe found a book with a rose on the cover. It was called *Sleeping Beauty*.
As she looked through the pages, she became convinced that the story was true.

When she saw that it was exactly 1000 years to the day since it was written she
took the book and ran from the library.

Off she rushed to the rose tree as fast as she could. She had just a few hours
until midnight to help Sleeping Beauty.

At the rose tree, Zoe fought her way through the vines, crawling over giant thorns and brushing aside enormous petals. Time ticked by and in the gloom Zoe was lost. Suddenly in the distance she saw a light. It was Flora's light and it led Zoe to the house hidden deep within the great rose.

Opening the door she was amazed at what she saw. "It's like a museum," she said, going into each room. On opening the last door, she saw the girl, asleep. "Sleeping Beauty," she whispered. As the clock began to strike midnight she reached out and touched the sleeping girl's hand.

As their fingers met, Annabel's eyes opened. "I feel like I've been asleep for ages," she said "I hope I haven't missed my 16th birthday."

Zoe stared at her "No, you haven't missed your birthday, but you are not 16. You are 1016! You are the youngest-looking oldest person ever!" she exclaimed.

Zoe sat down beside Annabel. She showed her the book and told her the whole tale. Annabel laughed and cried as she realised her life, as she knew it, was gone. She looked at the shining light and the rose tree that had once surrounded her house as it slowly receded to one small bud.

"Thank you my dear Aunts," she whispered,

"You've kept me safe for 1000 years."

Annabel's sadness turned to excitement and she ran to the door, desperate to see what the world was like. "Come on," she said, taking Zoe's hand "Show me the future," and they stepped out together into the bright morning sunshine.